SMALL
TO THE
RESCUE

First published in Great Britain by HarperCollins Children's Books in 2010.

1 3 5 7 9 10 8 6 4 2

ISBN: 978-0-00-731980-0

A CIP catalogue record for this title is available from the British Library.

The HarperCollins website address is www.harpercollins.co.uk

Based on the television series Big & Small and the original script, 'A Door for Small' by Jonathan Greenberg and Kathy Waugh.
Adapted for this publication by Davey Moore.

© Kindle Entertainment Limited 2010

Printed and bound in China

HarperCollins *Children's Books*

SMALL
TO THE
RESCUE

It was a quiet and peaceful morning in the house. Big was at the breakfast table pouring milk onto his cereal when -

CRASH!

A frying pan flew out of a kitchen cupboard.

CLANG!

A cheese grater came after the frying pan and that was followed by a small orange fist... holding a big purple feather!

'**Woo-hoo**' said Small, 'I've found my tickling feather! Now it's time to go and find the frogs!'

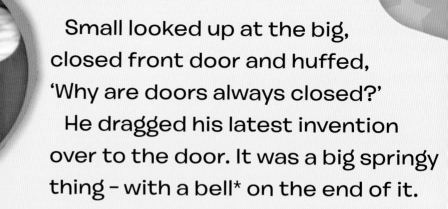

Small looked up at the big, closed front door and huffed, 'Why are doors always closed?' He dragged his latest invention over to the door. It was a big springy thing - with a bell* on the end of it.

* To make sure everyone gets out of the way when they hear it coming!

'What are you doing?'
Big wanted to know.
    'I'm opening the door!'
explained Small, climbing
on top of the springy thing.
    'That does not look safe,' said Big.

Small flew up towards the door and caught hold of the door handle! He turned the handle and the door swung open.

Small dropped down and landed on the doorstep outside. He waved cheerily to his friend, 'See you later, Big!' And he scooted off to the pond to go and tickle the frogs.

'I must make it easier for Small to get outside,' said Big. 'I think I'll make a new door, just for Small!'

Big found everything he needed and put on a hard hat, just in case. He drew on the wall, where he thought the small door should be.

It's a good idea to DRAW your door, before you BUILD your door. But the most important thing to remember is to be very, VERY precise!

Big put on some safety goggles, to protect his eyes.
And then he picked up his sledge hammer and -

KER-SMAAASSSH!

He knocked a hole through the wall.

Before long, Big was finishing off the doorway, making it nice and tidy around the edges. 'Not bad!' he said to himself, 'Not bad at all!'

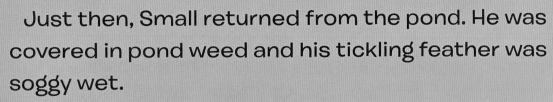

Just then, Small returned from the pond. He was covered in pond weed and his tickling feather was soggy wet.

'You know what?' said Small, 'Tickling frogs is harder than you think!'

'Hey, Small!' said Big, pointing at the small door.

'Not now,' said Small. 'I'm busy!'

Small went away for a minute and
came back with another invention -
his special rope plunger thingy.
He threw the plunger at the door
and climbed the rope.

'You don't have to do that!' said Big.

But Small was too busy climbing up the door.

He reached down and turned the door knob.

The door swung open and Small dropped down to the ground.

'Look, Small!' said Big,

'I made you a small door, just your size! It's just like a real door only teeny tiny!'

'Small?' said Small. 'Teeny tiny? What are you talking about? I fit in the big door just fine!'

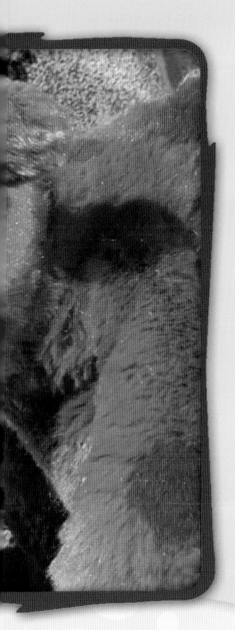

'I thought you'd like your own door,' said Big.

'Why do you think that I always need your help?' shouted Small. 'You should ask me for help some time and see how it feels.'

Small went through the big door in a big huff.

Big let out a heavy sigh. He didn't know why Small didn't like his special door. Maybe there was something wrong with it. He pushed his head through the new, little door.

It was a squeeze but he managed it, and his head popped out the other side.

'This is a great little door!' said Big.

He tried to pull his head back but he was stuck in the small door!

'Oh no,' said Big. He shouted for his friend.

When Small heard Big calling out for help, he sped over in his speedy blue car.

'Help me!' said Big, 'I'm stuck!' Small could hardly believe his ears.

'You need help from me?' asked Small.

'Yes, please,' said Big, quietly.

'**Woo-hoo**' said Small, excitedly. 'I'll have you out in no time!' And he sped off.

Almost instantly,
Small came back with his rope plunger thingy.

'Alright, Big,' said Small. 'It's a good job you asked me
to save you because I have a brilliant plan!'

Small stuck the plunger to Big's bottom and tied the
end of the rope to his car.

'Are you ready?' asked Small.

'No!' said Big.

'Then here we go!' said Small, and he started the car...

The wheels of the car spun round and round – but Small didn't go anywhere.

'I don't think it's working!' shouted Big, over the screeching of the car tyres on the kitchen floor.

Big didn't budge but – **POP!** – the plunger came away from Big's bottom. Small went speeding across the kitchen and – **KER-LANNNG!** – crashed his car into the wall on the other side.

'So much for my brilliant plan,' said Small, as the wheels fell off his car and rolled away.

The sun was setting over Big and Small's garden
and it was time for tea. Big was still stuck in the small
door and Small was feeding him noodles. Big sighed.

'Hey, Small,' said Big, 'I'm sorry I made you this little
door. I should have asked you first.'

'That's OK,' said Small. 'I'm sorry I don't have brilliant
plan number two.'

Small fed Big a forkful of noodles. Big chewed thoughtfully and then said, 'Hey, Small? Could you put some more butter on my noodles? They're not slurpy enough.'

'Butter!' said Small. 'THAT'S IT!'

Small went away and came back with a big stick of butter. He rubbed it around Big's neck. The butter made Big's neck all nice and slippy slurpy.

Small pushed and pushed. Big pulled and pulled. Small pushed some more. And Big pulled until...

POP!

Big pulled himself through the small door and fell back into the kitchen!

'You did it, Small!' cheered Big.

'Yay for me!' said Small, and he ran into the house.

'Hey, Small!' Big laughed, 'You just ran through your small door!'

'Oh, yeah!' said Small. 'Well, it's a good little door... even though I don't need it. But thanks anyway, Big.'

'Aw, you're welcome Small,' said Big.
And they both sighed, happily. Small knew he could use the small door if he wanted to - but Big had better stick to the big door in future!

THE QUITE BIG BOOK ABOUT BIG

THE NOT SO SMALL BOOK ABOUT SMALL

Smallish Library

MEET BIG MEET SMALL

QUICK, QUICK, SNOW!

THE MYSTERIOUS WOODS

BIG AND SMALL'S Busiest Day Ever
A sticky sticker storybook

Includes CD

SINGALONG SONG BOOK

WOWZARAMA DOODLE BOOK